TODAY!

WOW!

FUN FACTS
AHEAD!

MEET

THE

PANGOLIN

I Am NOT a Penguin

by Liz Wong

Alfred A. Knopf

New York

Meet the Pangolin!

Pangolins are mammals that are covered with scales.

Pangolins live in Asia and Africa.

Of course, if I need to protect myself, I can curl up into a ball.

Oh, I get it! He's an armadillo.

Y'all talking about armadillos?

LISTEN UP! I'M A PANGOLIN! I'M NOT A FROG, NOT A SNAKE, NOT A SKUNK, NOT AN ANTEATER, NOT A BEAR, AND NOT AN ARMADILLO! I AM CERTAINLY NOT A PENGUIN! I DON'T WANT TO TALK ABOUT PENGUINS! THERE ARE NO PENGUINS HERE! ZERO PENGUINS! **NOT. ONE. PENGUIN!**

Huff
Huff

There are eight species of pangolin. Four species live in Asia, and four species live in Africa.

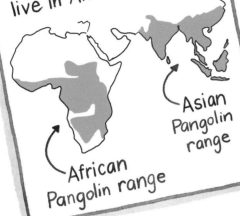

African Pangolin range

Asian Pangolin range

Pangolins are often called "scaly anteaters," but, in fact, they are more closely related to bears than anteaters.

Most species of pangolins live on the ground in burrows, but some live in trees. They are solitary creatures, who usually sleep rolled up in a ball during the day and are active at night.

Pangolins are the only mammals that are covered with scales. Scales cover most of their bodies, except the sides of their faces and their underbellies, which have a little fur.

Pangolin scales are made of keratin. Keratin is the same material that makes up our hair and fingernails. The edges of their scales can be very sharp.

Pangolins are endangered. They are hunted for their meat and scales, and are also threatened by habitat loss.

A baby pangolin is called a pangopup and rides on its mother's tail until it is about three months old.

Pangolins don't have teeth. They swallow small stones that help to grind up food in their stomachs.

Pangolins use the sharp claws on their front feet to dig into ant and termite nests and slurp up the insects with their long, sticky tongues. A pangolin can eat nearly 200,000 ants a day!

To defend themselves, pangolins roll up into a ball. They can also release a stinky liquid from a gland under their tail.

Pangolins have poor eyesight, but have sharp senses of smell and hearing.

The word *pangolin* comes from the Malay word *pengguling*, which means "one who rolls up."